Karen's Home Run

Look for these
and other books about Karen
in the
Baby-sitters Little Sister series:

1 Karen's Witch

2 Karen's Roller Skates

3 Karen's Worst Day

4 Karen's Kittycat Club

5 Karen's School Picture

6 Karen's Little Sister

7 Karen's Birthday

8 Karen's Haircut

9 Karen's Sleepover

#10 Karen's Grandmothers

#11 Karen's Prize

#12 Karen's Ghost

#13 Karen's Surprise

#14 Karen's New Year

#15 Karen's in Love

#16 Karen's Goldfish

#17 Karen's Brothers

#18 Karen's Home Run

#19 Karen's Good-bye

Super Special:
1 Karen's Wish

Little Sister

Karen's Home Run

Ann M. Martin

Illustrations by Susan Tang

A
LITTLE APPLE
PAPERBACK

SCHOLASTIC INC.
New York Toronto London Auckland Sydney

ISBN 0-590-43642-2

12 11 10 9 8 7 6 5 4 3 2 1   1 2 3 4 5 6/9

Printed in the U.S.A.   40

First Scholastic printing, May 1991

This book is for four fans in Maine,
Emily, Rebecca, Laura, and Peter,
with love from Ann.

Karen's Home Run

Kristy's Krushers

"Hello, everybody! I'm home!"

"Hi, sweetie. We're in the kitchen," answered Mommy.

I dropped my book bag on the floor. I ran into our kitchen. There were Mommy and Andrew. They were baking something. Andrew was wearing an apron. He is my little brother. He is four, going on five. And I am his big sister, Karen Brewer. I just turned seven.

Andrew and I both have blond hair. We

have some freckles, too. And we have blue eyes. But I am the only one of us who wears glasses. I even have two pairs. One pair is for reading. Those glasses are blue. The other pair is for the rest of the time. They are pink. (I do not have to wear the pink glasses when I am asleep, of course.)

"How was school?" Mommy asked me.

"Fine."

"Did you drop your book bag on the floor when you came in?"

I am not supposed to do that. I thought about saying no. But Mommy would find the bag and then I would be in trouble. Not gigundo trouble. Just teensy trouble. I decided to tell the truth. It is always safer to do that.

"Yes," I said to Mommy. And before she could open her mouth, I ran out of the kitchen. I picked up my book bag. I stuck it in the closet. I put it right next to my softball glove and Andrew's catcher's mitt.

"Hey, Andrew," I said when I returned

to the kitchen. "We have a Krushers practice today. Are you ready?"

"I guess," replied my brother. He did not look at me.

"What's wrong?" I asked him.

"All the other kids on our team are playing better. Except me."

"Andrew, that is not true."

Andrew shrugged.

My brother and I play on a softball team. The team is called Kristy's Krushers. Guess who Kristy is. She is our big stepsister. I love her so, so much. And she is a very good softball coach. There are a whole bunch of kids on our team. Kristy teaches us lots of things. She is patient. We do not always play too well. But Kristy does not get mad at us.

Kristy does not even get mad when we lose a game to Bart's Bashers. The Bashers are the enemy team. They are kids, like us. But they are a little older. And they are better players. Usually, the Krushers lose when they play a game against the Bashers. We try hard, but we lose.

By the way, Bart, the Bashers' coach, is Kristy's boyfriend. (Hee, hee, hee.)

"Andrew," I said. "You're playing better, too. You are a very good catcher now. And before, you could hardly ever catch the ball. Remember?"

"I am not a good hitter, though," Andrew replied.

Well, that was true. Andrew was not a good hitter. But maybe he could be if he practiced.

"You would be a better hitter if you practiced," I said.

"I don't know."

"I could help you practice. I could toss balls to you in the backyard. We could practice every day after school. Or almost every day."

"Karen, that is a very nice offer," spoke up Mommy. She was untying Andrew's apron.

4

"Thank you," I replied.

"Are you ready to go?" asked Mommy.

"Yup," I said. Andrew and I were as ready as we would ever be.

"Okay then, kids. Get your things together and climb in the car."

The Parade

I was sitting in the outfield. I was making a chain of clovers. See, what you do is pick one clover. Then you slit the stem with your thumb just below the flower. And then you stick another clover through the slit. After that, you —

"Karen!" called Kristy. "Are you paying attention?"

"Not really," I answered. I never pay attention when I am in the outfield. That is because the Krushers hardly ever hit the ball that far. But I knew that I should *look* like I was paying attention. So I stood up. Soon I began singing songs under my breath. At least that was something to do.

Being in the outfield is gigundo boring.

"Okay, Andrew!" I heard Kristy say. "Keep your eye on the ball."

I dropped the clover chain. I squinted my eyes and looked across the field. Andrew was at bat. I had to see how he would do.

Jackie Rodowsky was pitching. Jackie is seven. He is very, very nice. And Kristy likes him. But she calls him a walking disaster. That means that he is always causing accidents. He does not mean to, though.

Jackie pitched a low, slow ball to Andrew. It was a good pitch. Andrew tried for the ball, but he missed it by a mile. And then, as he was swinging the bat around, he let go of it. It flew through the air. Luckily, nobody got hurt.

"Andrew!" Kristy cried. "What happened? Remember — if you don't hit the ball, hold onto the bat. If you do hit the ball, *drop* the bat. Do not let it fly."

"I'm sorry," said Andrew in a quivery voice. "I didn't mean to throw the bat. It just slipped out of my hands."

"That's okay," replied Kristy. "Go ahead, you have two more tries."

Jackie pitched two more easy balls. Andrew missed both of them. And the bat flew out of his hands each time. Nobody, not even Kristy, was standing near Andrew anymore. A bunch of kids had run behind the backstop, where they would be protected.

"Three strikes!" called Kristy. "And that was three outs. The game is over!"

We ran off the field. I ran straight to Andrew. I saw tears in his eyes.

"I made my side lose the game," he said to me. "I am a horrible player."

"No, you're not. You are a very good catcher. You just need to practice hitting — and holding onto the bat," I told him.

"Karen!" I heard someone call. I turned around. It was Hannie Papadakis. Hannie is a Krusher, too. And she is one of my best friends. (I have two best friends. The other is Nancy Dawes. She is not a Krusher. Hannie and Nancy and I are in Ms. Colman's second-grade class at Stoneybrook Academy. We call ourselves the Three Musketeers.)

Some of my other friends are on the team, too. Well, one of them is actually my stepbrother. He is seven, like me. He is Kristy's brother, and his name is David Michael. Plus, I know lots of the girl players. And I know our three cheerleaders. Let me see. Who else is on the team? Linny Papadakis (Hannie's older brother), and Max Delaney. I am a friend of Max's sister, Amanda.

"Karen," said Hannie again. "Kristy wants to talk to us."

The Krushers crowded around my sister.

"Good news," said Kristy. "We are going to march in the Memorial Day parade next month. The Bashers will march, too." (Ooh, I thought. Marching in a parade! I just love having people look at me.) *"And,"*

Kristy went on, "on the day before Memorial Day, we will play a big game against the Bashers. The winning team will get to carry a special banner in the parade. But whether we have the banner or not, the Krushers are going to look good. We will have our Krushers T-shirts and hats. And guess what. Our new batting gloves will arrive soon. We can wear those in the parade, too."

"Yea!" shouted the Krushers. Except for Andrew. What he said was, "Karen? Will we be at the big house or the little house on Memorial Day?"

3

Special Days

"We will be at the big house on Memorial Day," I told Andrew.

"Is Memorial Day a *very* important holiday?" he asked.

"Yes," I replied. "But it is not special like Thanksgiving or Easter. At least not in our family. For some families it is special, though."

"But not for ours," Andrew repeated. "Good. Then there won't be any fighting."

"I don't think so."

What Andrew meant about the fighting

is that our parents are divorced. And *some*-times they fight over us. But not too often.

Daddy lives in a big house here in Stoneybrook, Connecticut. It is the house he grew up in. Mommy and Andrew and I used to live there, too. But then my parents got divorced. They were not mad at each other. They just decided that they did not love each other anymore. So Mommy moved into a little house that is also in Stoneybrook. Most of the time, Andrew and I live at the little house. But every other weekend, and for two weeks during the summer, we live at the big house. And we split up the holidays. Or else we have two of each holiday. That is when Mommy and Daddy fight sometimes. Mommy would like us to celebrate each holiday with her. And Daddy would like us to celebrate each holiday with him. But I did not think that they would fight about Memorial Day.

Do you want to know something interesting? Mommy and Daddy each got married again. So Andrew and I have a stepfather and a stepmother now. We have two families, one at each house. Here are the people and pets who live at the little house: Mommy, Seth (my stepfather), Rocky and Midgie (Seth's cat and dog), and Emily Junior (my rat). And, of course, Andrew and me.

Here are the people and pets who live at the big house: Daddy, Elizabeth (my stepmother), Elizabeth's four kids — Charlie, Sam, Kristy, and David Michael — Nannie (Elizabeth's mother), Emily Michelle, Boo-Boo, Shannon, Goldfishie, Crystal Light the Second, and sometimes Andrew and me. I have already told you about Kristy and David Michael. Charlie and Sam are their older brothers. They go to high school. Emily Michelle is my adopted sister. She is two and a half. Daddy and Elizabeth adopted her from a country called Vietnam. (I named my rat after Emily.) Nannie came to live at the big house not long after Emily arrived. She takes care of Emily while Daddy and Elizabeth are at work. Boo-Boo is Daddy's old, fat cat. Shannon is David Michael's puppy. Goldfishie is Andrew's goldfish. Crystal Light the Second is my goldfish.

I call my brother Andrew Two-Two. I call myself Karen Two-Two. (I got the name from a book Ms. Colman read to our class. It was called *Jacob Two-Two Meets the Hooded Fang*.) I think "Two-Two" is a good name for Andrew and me. It is a good name because we have two of so many things. We have two houses, two families, two mommies, two daddies, two cats, and two dogs. And I have two stuffed cats. Moosie stays at the big house, Goosie stays at the little house. Andrew and I have clothes and toys at each house. Plus, Nancy Dawes lives next door to the little house, and Hannie Papadakis lives across the street and one house down from the big house.

Of course, Andrew and I do not have two of *everything*. For instance, there is only one Kristy. I miss her a lot when I am at Mommy's. And there is only one Emily Junior.

I miss *her* when I am at Daddy's. (Also, Mommy has to take care of Emily Junior when I am at the big house. She is not wild about this, but what can you do?)

Our Krushers practice was over. Kristy had finished talking to us. Parents and baby-sitters were starting to arrive. It was time for Andrew and me to go back to the little house.

The Junk Bucket

"Karen?" said Andrew. "How many days until the big game?"

"The big game?" I repeated. "You mean against the Bashers?"

Andrew nodded.

Well, for heaven's sake, I did not know. "Andrew, the game isn't until next month," I said. "I would have to count the days on a calendar."

It was a Saturday. Andrew and I were at the big house for the weekend. We had been practicing Andrew's hitting in the backyard. It was a good thing the yard is big. Andrew let his bat fly *every* time he swung at the ball. Once, the bat crashed into a tree.

"Are you already nervous about the game?" I asked my brother.

"Yup," he answered.

"Then think about the parade the next day. It will be almost as much fun as the softball game. Think of our batting gloves. We will have them by then."

"Yeah . . ." said Andrew slowly.

"Karen! Andrew! Time for lunch!" Elizabeth was calling to us from the back door of the big house.

"Coming!" we shouted to her.

Andrew and I ran inside. Our brothers and sisters were gathering in the kitchen. Daddy and Elizabeth were taking things out of the refrigerator. Nannie was already sitting at the table. She was talking to Emily in her high chair.

Soon everyone was seated. We were eating sandwiches and salad. (Charlie was eating the most. I have never seen anyone eat as much as he does.)

"Guess what," said Sam. "I forgot to tell you this yesterday. Our band is going to march in the Memorial Day parade." (Sam plays the clarinet in the high-school band. He is pretty good.)

"Cool," I said. "Will you wear uniforms?"

"Yup." Sam nodded.

"I guess we're all going to be in the parade then," said Kristy.

"Really? Our whole family?" asked Andrew.

"Well, all the kids," replied Kristy. "You and Karen and David Michael and I will march with the Krushers, and now Sam will be marching with the band."

"What about Charlie and Emily?" I asked.

"Oh. I guess you didn't hear," said Charlie. "Last week the coach decided that our cheerleaders should be in the parade. Usually the team members get to march and the cheerleaders — who cheer for *all* our teams — are forgotten. So the coach asked me to drive them in my car this year."

Charlie looked proud, but I said, "In the *Junk* Bucket?"

"Yes, in the Junk Bucket."

"We're going to help Charlie decorate it," spoke up Kristy. "And Emily is going to ride with Charlie. He's going to say she's the cheerleaders' mascot. We'll have to make a really good costume for Emily."

"Fun," I said. "We all get to march *and* be in costume. Oh, wait. Charlie, will you be dressed as anything special?"

"A football player," he said.

"Perfect!" I exclaimed.

"Boy," added Daddy. "I better make sure I've got tape in my camcorder. I want to film the entire parade. I want to get a shot of each of you."

"In our uniforms," I said.

"Yes, in your uniforms," agreed Daddy.

Goody. I could not wait for the batting gloves to arrive. I wanted to see myself in my entire Krushers uniform!

The Bicycle Brigade

On Sunday, I went over to Amanda Delaney's house. Amanda lives across the street from the big house. There is one house between hers and Hannie's. Amanda and Hannie are gigundo enemies. But Amanda and I are friends. We are friends even though Amanda is older than I am, and even though she goes to Stoneybrook Day School instead of Stoneybrook Academy.

Amanda has a swimming pool.

I usually only get to see Amanda on big-house weekends.

When I rang the Delaneys' bell, Amanda's mother answered the door.

"Hi, Karen," she said.

"Hi!" I answered. "Is Amanda here?"

"She's in the backyard. You can scoot on through, if you want."

Mrs. Delaney meant that I could scoot on through the house and go out the back door. Which I did.

I saw Amanda sitting on the lawn. Her bicycle was next to her. It was propped up on its kickstand. Around Amanda were streamers, crepe paper, Scotch tape, scissors, and some other stuff.

"Hi, Amanda! What are you doing?" I called.

Amanda got up quickly. She stood in front of her bicycle. She looked as if she were trying to hide it. "Who let you out here?" she demanded.

Sheesh. Sometimes I can see why Hannie

doesn't like Amanda. "Your mom did," I replied. "What are you doing?"

Amanda did not answer my question. Instead she muttered something like, "I *told* my mother I wanted to work alone. I never have any privacy."

Since I did not leave, Amanda said, "Oh, all right. You might as well know. I'm going to ride in the Bicycle Brigade in the Memorial Day parade. And I bet I will win first prize."

"What's first prize?" I asked. "And what's the Bicycle Brigade?"

"Oh," said Amanda. "This year, any kid who wants to can decorate his bicycle and ride at the end of the parade. A judge will look at the bicycles and choose three winners. First prize is . . . one hundred dollars."

"Wow," I said softly.

"So that's why I don't want you out here," Amanda told me. "I don't want you to see what I'm doing."

Amanda meant, "I don't want you to

steal my ideas." So I said to her proudly, "You don't have to worry about me, Amanda. *I* will be marching with the Krushers. And we should have our batting gloves by then, so our uniforms will be great: T-shirts, hats, and gloves. And some kids will carry bats and mitts. I would rather march with my team than be stuck with my bike at the end of the parade." I smiled sweetly at Amanda.

"Yeah? Well, I would like to win a hundred dollars," said Amanda. "Wouldn't you?"

"Of course. But the Krushers need me."

Amanda just went on working. She tied plastic streamers to the end of her handle-bars. She wove crepe paper through the spokes of her wheels.

Finally I asked, "What are second prize and third prize?"

Amanda grinned. "Second prize is fifty dollars. Third prize is a free giant ice-cream sundae at Sullivan's Sweets."

"Wow," I couldn't help saying. Those

Home Run!

At our next Krushers practice, Kristy did what she usually does. First she gave us a pep talk. Then we practiced pitching, hitting, and catching the ball. And *then* Kristy divided us into two teams: Krushers 1 and Krushers 2.

We played a short game against each other. Andrew and I were both on the Krushers 2 team. We like playing on the same side.

But Andrew did not play very well that day. The first time he went to bat, David

Michael pitched the ball to him. It was a good pitch. Andrew swung at it. He did not hit the ball.

Also, he let his bat fly again. No one was hurt. No one was standing anywhere near my brother. Not even the catcher. The catcher was Hannie, and she had told Kristy that she would not catch when Andrew was at bat.

As the bat sailed through the air, Andrew watched it.

"Bullfrogs!" he shouted. He stamped his foot.

"Andrew!" exclaimed Kristy. But then all she added was, "Strike one. Go get your bat."

Andrew found the bat. David Michael pitched to him again. Andrew swung. He let go of the bat and it landed somewhere near left field.

A couple of kids laughed.

But Kristy was not even smiling. "Andrew," she said, "*hold onto* the bat. Never let it fly. If you hit the ball, then just *drop* the bat, okay?"

"*Okay!*" Andrew looked like he might cry. "I know I'm supposed to do that. But I can't help it."

"Do you want to hit again?" asked Kristy. "You only have — "

"NO!" cried Andrew. "I'm finished." He laid his bat on the ground so gently and carefully that it took him about five minutes.

"Don't worry, Andrew," I said. "Nobody hits the ball every time."

"Karen! You're up next!" called Kristy.

"Okay." I ran to home plate. I picked up the bat Andrew had been using. "Ready or not, David Michael!" I shouted.

David Michael wound up and pitched the ball. He pitched it much faster than when he had pitched to Andrew.

I kept my eyes on the ball. When the time seemed right, I swung the bat. Hard.

WHACK! I hit the ball! I could not even

see where it went. That was how fast it was flying. "Boy . . . " I said softly.

"Run, Karen!" Kristy cried.

I ran. I touched first base, second base, third base, and finally I was running across home plate.

"Home run!" shouted Kristy.

Everyone began to cheer for me. Even the kids on Krushers 1. I had hit the ball *so* hard that we could not even find it.

Now, I thought, I will *really* be happy to march with the Krushers. Maybe my teammates would even start calling me Home Run Karen or something.

I glanced at Andrew. He was sitting alone on the bleachers. His head was in his hands. When the game ended, he was still sitting that way. I tried to make him feel better. "You just had a bad day," I said.

"I always have bad days," he replied.

"Oh, that is not so," I told him. But I was thinking about something else. I was thinking about our big game against the Bashers. I was ready for it.

Roller Blades and Nintendo

A few days later, I was in Ms. Colman's room, waiting for my teacher to start class. Most of us kids were in the room. But Ms. Colman was not. So I stood around with Hannie and Nancy.

Everyone was talking.

They were talking about the Bicycle Brigade.

"I am going to win first prize," said Hank Reubens. "You guys will never guess what I'm doing to my bicycle. It will be so, so cool."

"What are you doing?" I asked.

"I can't tell you, Karen!" Hank exclaimed. "Then everyone would copy me. Well, I will tell you this much: I need *batteries*."

"My bicycle will be making noise," said Natalie Springer.

"So will mine," said Bobby Gianelli. "*And* I need a lot of fake fur. You know, like those coonskin hats."

"Well, I am not going to say a thing about my bicycle," spoke up Pamela Harding. (Pamela and I do not like each other.)

"That's because your head is empty," said Bobby. "I bet you don't have any ideas yet."

"Wrong, birdbrain," replied Pamela. "I'm almost done decorating my bike. It will win the one hundred dollars. And when it does, I am going to buy a pair of roller blades."

"No, you're not," said Hank. "Because *I* am going to win the money and buy roller blades."

"If I won," said Bobby, "I would buy lots of CDs."

Nancy turned to me. "Karen?" she said. "What would you do with a hundred dollars? . . . A *hun*dred dollars?"

"I'm not riding in the Bicycle Brigade," I told her. "I'm marching with the Krushers. So are Andrew and Kristy and David Michael and Hannie."

"But just pretend. *If* you had a hundred dollars, what would you buy?"

"I know what I'd buy," said Natalie. "A whole bunch of jigsaw puzzles."

Natalie is such a drip.

"Hey, Ricky!" I called. (Ricky Torres and I got married once. He is my husband.) "What would you buy?"

"Roller blades. No, Nintendo games. Definitely Nintendo games."

Roller blades and Nintendo games sure sounded like fun.

Loser

I was standing in the outfield again.

I was daydreaming.

In my daydream, I could see myself with a new pair of roller blades. They were gigundo fancy. They were silver with shiny green wheels. I flew along a street. I coasted down a hill. . . .

"Karen!" Kristy was shouting. "Are you paying attention?"

I guess I was not. If I had been paying attention, I would have seen that the other team had struck out. The Krushers were changing sides. I was not supposed to be in the outfield anymore. I was supposed to be in the batting lineup with the kids on Krushers 2.

"Sorry," I yelled to Kristy. I ran off the field. I took my place behind Andrew. "What's the score?" I whispered to him.

"Five to four," he answered. "We're winning."

"Good," I said.

But the Krushers 1 pitcher didn't let the first three Krushers 2 hitters get any runs. And now it was Andrew's turn at bat.

"Hold onto it!" I said to my brother. "Do not let go of the bat."

Andrew set his mouth in a straight line. He looked like he planned to hit a home run.

The pitcher threw the ball.

It was a terrible throw, but Andrew swung at it anyway.

He missed — and he let the bat go flying.

Suddenly I noticed something awful. A man was standing on the edge of the softball diamond. He was watching our practice. Now Andrew's bat was sailing toward his head.

"DUCK, MISTER!" I yelled at the top of my lungs.

The man ducked. The bat missed him by inches.

"Andrew!" Kristy exclaimed. "I want to talk to you later."

The man exclaimed something, too. "I'm getting out of here!"

He left.

I was up at bat. But I was not keeping my eye on the ball. I was not concentrating. First I thought about Andrew and the bat and the man. Then I thought about silver-and-green roller blades. Before I knew it, I had struck out.

My side did not get any more runs. The other side did, though. So when I went to bat the next time, I *knew* I should pay attention. But I couldn't. I could not stop imagining myself on those roller blades.

"Strike three, you're out!" Kristy announced. "Game's over. Practice is over. The Krushers One won this game. Good work, everybody!"

The Krushers 1 had won? That meant I had lost the game for us. What kind of teammate was I? A horrible one, that's what. A loser.

I carried the bat to Kristy. Kristy was talking to Andrew. "It's getting dangerous to let you play," she was saying. (I could tell she felt bad.) But my mind was not on Andrew or Kristy or flying bats.

"Kristy?" I said when she finished talking with Andrew. "I have to tell you something. I cannot march with the Krushers in the parade. I am a loser."

"Are you kidding, Karen?" said Kristy. "Are you sure you're not mad because I talked to Andrew and he is crying?"

"Nope. I'm just a loser. I do not deserve to march with the Krushers."

"But everybody makes mistakes. Remember what happened to Andrew last week?"

I remembered. But I did not care. I had never lost a game for my team before. I felt awful.

When Mommy picked up Andrew and me that afternoon, we were both crying.

Don't Give Up

Kristy called me at the little house that night. "Karen," she said, "I will feel very sad if you don't march with the Krushers."

"Why?" I asked. "I struck out. I lost the game for my team."

"And you are not the first person to make a mistake. That's one reason I started the Krushers. So you guys could have fun and play softball and not feel embarrassed."

"But I — "

"The Krushers are not quitters," Kristy

reminded me. "Please don't give up, Karen. I'll miss you if you do. And so will the rest of the team."

"No, they won't," I replied. "No one will miss someone who strikes out and loses games."

"All right," said Kristy. "Listen. Think this over for awhile. Don't make up your mind yet. You might wake up tomorrow feeling like a champion player."

"I doubt it," I said. "But I will think about it. I'll let you know soon."

"Okay." Kristy hung up the phone. She sounded sad already.

The next evening, Mommy and Seth came into my room. I was doing some homework. (Ms. Colman gives us homework and we are only in *second* grade.)

Mommy sat on my bed. Seth sat next to her.

"Is something wrong?" I asked. (I am pretty used to being in trouble.)

"We hear that you don't want to march

in the Memorial Day parade with the rest of the Krushers," Mommy told me.

"Who said?" I demanded.

"It doesn't matter. We think you're being too hard on yourself."

"Much too hard," added Seth.

"I can't help it. Besides, I am still thinking. *Maybe* I will march with the Krushers."

"We hope so," said Mommy.

"Everyone would be very proud of you," said Seth.

Even Andrew talked to me about what I was doing. "I'm a *terrible* player," he said. "Kristy might not let me play in the game against the Bashers, since I might hurt someone. But I'm still going to march with our team."

"So?" I was beginning to feel angry.

"All right," said Andrew. "But if you don't walk with us, what *will* you do on Memorial Day? All our brothers and sisters will be in the parade."

"I'll watch," I snapped. "Someone has to watch."

"Okay-ay," sang Andrew. He walked out of my room.

I was mad. What Andrew had said was true. If I did not march with the Krushers, I would be the only kid in *both* of my families who was not in the parade. And I wanted to be in the parade very badly.

I flopped onto my bed. I thought about the Krushers. I thought about the parade. I thought about roller blades. And then I thought about . . . the Bicycle Brigade!

I could be in the parade after all! I would even have a chance at winning one hundred dollars. Then I could buy silver-and-green roller blades.

But then I thought, Uh-oh. If I ride in the Bicycle Brigade, will my friends think I am being greedy? Will they think I deserted the Krushers just so I could win some money? And did I want to compete against Amanda and Ricky and all my friends?

I did not know.

10

Karen's Choice

By the next day I did not know any more than I had known the night before. I had thought and thought and thought about my choice. But I had no answers. Did I deserve to march with the Krushers? Should I risk riding in the Bicycle Brigade? After I thought some more, I began to wonder about something.

How did I know if I was good enough to ride in the brigade? After all, the kids in my class needed batteries and all sorts of things to decorate their bikes. What could

45

I do that would be just as good?

I would have to experiment.

I found paper, scissors, glue, crepe paper, clothespins, and some old baseball cards. I took everything into the garage. Then I sat down next to my little-house bicycle.

"Hmm," I said.

I picked up the roll of pink crepe paper. I wound the paper around my handlebars. That looked very beautiful.

Then I fastened baseball cards to the spokes of the wheels. I held them in place with the clothespins. I moved my bike back and forth.

BRRRRR went the wheels!

"Nice sound effect," I said.

I sat down again. I looked at my baskets. I looked at the colored paper. I thought that paper butterflies on the bike baskets would be gigundo pretty.

I was trying to figure out how to make butterflies when a voice called, "Karen!"

I whirled around.

Nancy was standing in the doorway to the garage.

"What are you doing?" she asked.

"Um." (I know I was blushing.) "I'm deciding whether I want to ride in the Bicycle Brigade on Memorial Day."

"But how *could* you? You're a Krusher. You're supposed to march with your team. Plus, *I'm* going to ride in the brigade. I don't want to compete against you."

"I don't want to compete against you, either," I said in a small voice. "Or Amanda or Ricky or Natalie or anyone."

"So march with the Krushers. Does Kristy know you're thinking about riding in the brigade?"

"No," I whispered.

"I just don't get it," said Nancy. She crossed her arms.

"Well, I don't think I deserve to march with the Krushers," I told her. "I'm a loser. And anyway, when did *you* decide to ride in the parade? You never said you were going to do that."

"It was a secret."

"Why?"

Nancy shrugged. "Just because."

"You know, you can't make me march with the Krushers."

"Did I say I could?" asked Nancy.

"No. . . . But you don't look very happy."

"Well, I'm not. You're a greedy-guts, Karen!" (This was not the first time I had been called that.) "You are supposed to walk with your softball team in the parade. But you are going to desert them. You just want to win the prize money."

"That's not true!" I cried. "I want to be in the parade, that's all. I mean, I *would* like a hundred dollars — "

"*See?*" shouted Nancy. (Nancy almost never gets angry.) "Good-bye, Karen!"

"*Good! Bye!* And don't steal my baseball-card idea."

"That is so lame," Nancy called over her shoulder. "Everyone knows how to do that."

Boo.

Karen's Jinx

I felt worse than ever. I did not think I should march with the Krushers. I was not a good enough player. Oh, sure. I had hit a home run. And Andrew was not a good player at all. Neither were lots of the Krushers. But they didn't lose entire games for their sides. Well, Andrew had. But not because he was daydreaming. You are not supposed to daydream when you play softball.

And now I did not really want to ride in

the Bicycle Brigade, either. I did not want to be called a greedy-guts. I did not want Nancy to be mad at me. And I certainly did not want to ride a "lame" bicycle.

But I did want to be in the parade.

I sighed. Then I took all the stuff off my bike. I carried the things into the little house, and I put them away.

Andrew was inside. He was looking through a picture book. When he saw me, he stopped. "Karen? I'm bored," he said. "Would you help me with my hitting? I really need practice."

"Okay. Let's find the bat and ball. We can practice in the backyard."

"Goody!" exclaimed Andrew. "Goody, goody gumdrops!"

In the backyard, Andrew stood ready with the bat. I stood opposite him with the softball.

I was wearing a football helmet. It was to protect me from flying bats.

"Okay, Andrew! Batting stance!"

Andrew got ready.

"Hold onto the bat!" I yelled. "Now. Here comes the ball."

I pitched an easy one to Andrew. He swung and missed. The bat took off. It sailed into our fence.

"Get the pets inside!" I cried. If Andrew could not control the bat, then Rocky and Midgie should not be around. So Andrew and I found them and put them in the house. Then Andrew got ready to swing at another ball.

"DO. NOT. LET. GO. OF. THE. BAT!" I screeched.

"Okay, okay."

But guess what happened. Andrew let the bat fly again. (Of course.) This time it sailed through Seth's flower garden. It landed somewhere beyond the garden. Andrew and I could not even see it.

We ran to the garden. "Andrew! You have killed a peony!" I exclaimed.

My brother looked at the peony plant. Its

one huge pink blossom lay in the dirt. "Uh-oh," said Andrew.

"You better tell Mommy," I said.

"Do I have to?"

"Yup."

I found the bat. Andrew and I headed for the house. Before we reached the back door, Mommy opened it. "Karen! Phone for you!" she called.

So I ran to pick up the phone, while Andrew told Mommy what he had done.

"Hi, it's Kristy," said the voice at the other end of the line. "I just wanted to let you and Andrew know that our next practice will actually be a trial game against the Bashers. You know, to get everybody warmed up."

"But, Kristy. I'm a jinx on the Krushers," I said.

"You are not!"

I didn't believe Kristy. I decided something, though. I decided that I would play in the trial game against the Bashers. If I did well, then I would play in the big game. I would march in the parade with the Krushers, too.

If I did not play well, then I would not do either thing.

Princess Emily

"They're he-ere!" I could hear Kristy call.

"They're here?" was David Michael's excited answer.

"Really?" asked Andrew.

It was a big-house weekend. It was Saturday morning. The mail had just been delivered. And I was pretty sure I knew what had arrived.

The Krushers batting gloves.

I left my room. I crossed the hall and looked through the rails of the banister. Below me, in the front hall, were crowded

Kristy, David Michael, and Andrew. They were ripping open a box.

"Batting gloves!" exclaimed David Michael. "They came at last. We can wear them in the practice game and the real game and then in the parade."

"Hurray!" cried Andrew. "Maybe they will help me with my hitting."

And Kristy said, "I better call the other Krushers. They'll want to know."

"I'm going to put on my whole uniform," said David Michael. "I want to see how everything looks together."

"Me, too," said Andrew.

The boys clattered upstairs.

"Batting gloves are here!" called Andrew as he ran by my room.

"Yea," I said. I went downstairs to see what was going on in the front yard. I knew that Sam and Charlie and their friends were working on the Junk Bucket. The parade was not for two weeks and two days. But the boys said they needed to plan ahead.

"What are you doing?" I asked Sam.

"We're trying to figure out how to make the Junk Bucket look like a giant grasshopper," he said.

"How come?"

"We just thought it would be funny. . . . Hey, Charlie! I've got an idea. Make the headlights look like eyes!"

"Oh, gross," I said. I went back into the house. Kristy was on the phone. She was calling the Krushers about the batting gloves. I sat at the kitchen table and listened.

When Kristy was finished, she said, "Want to help me put together a costume for Emily? She needs something for the parade."

"How about a grasshopper suit?" I suggested.

Kristy gave me a funny look. "I was thinking more along the lines of a princess," she replied. "Come on. Let's find Emily."

So we did. We took her up to the playroom, and we opened the box of dress-up clothes. Emily peeped inside. "Tinky," she announced.

"They're not stinky!" I cried. (*Stinky* is Emily's favorite new word.)

Kristy poked around in the box. She pulled out a frilly white dress.

"Tinky!" said Emily.

Kristy pulled out a sparkly wand and a very beautiful silver crown.

"Tinky!" said Emily.

"No, *pretty*," I exclaimed.

"Let's try this stuff on you," said Kristy. She slipped the dress over Emily's head. She handed her the wand. Then she put the crown in place.

"Perfect!" said Kristy.

"Princess Emily!" I announced.

"Tinky!" cried Emily.

A Real Team

Emily did not really think her costume was tinky. In fact, she would not let Kristy take it off her.

"Okay, then," said Kristy. "Let's go outside and show you to Charlie. Are you coming with us, Karen?"

I shook my head. All anybody could talk about today was softball and the parade. I did not want to think about either one. And I still thought I was a jinx on the Krushers. What if I played really badly in the trial game against the Bashers?

Maybe I should talk to Nannie. Nannie is a good listener and a good thinker. Also, she was not going to be in the parade. Maybe she could tell me what I should do.

"Nannie?" I called.

"In my room, Karen," she answered.

I ran to Nannie's room. "Hey, Nannie — " I started to say. Then I stopped. Nannie was sitting on the edge of her bed. All around her were patches and bowling trophies and bowling shirts, plus some pieces of white cardboard, some stakes, and a fat blue Magic Marker.

"What's all that stuff?" I asked.

Nannie grinned. "I just found out that my bowling team is going to march in the Memorial Day parade."

"It is?"

Nannie nodded. "When we won our last game, we became the senior-citizen bowling champions of Stoneybrook."

Boy, I thought. That's who should be in parades. Champions — not losers like me. I began to worry all over again about the

Krushers and the Bicycle Brigade and the trial game. Before I got too far, though, Nannie said, "Would you like to help me with some things?"

"Okay. What kind of things?"

"Getting-ready-for-the-parade things. I need to sew these patches onto one of my bowling shirts. Then I have to make some funny signs for my team members to carry in the parade."

"Oh." I did *not* want to help with parade stuff, but I had already told Nannie that I would.

First we sewed the patches onto one of the shirts. I am not bad at sewing.

Then we thought up things to write on the signs. Here's what we decided on: STONEYBROOK BOWLING CHAMPS!; SENIORS MAKE GOOD BOWLERS; GRAY POWER!; and, WE MAY BE OLD BUT WE CAN BOWL. I was disappointed that we didn't come up with any sayings that rhymed. But Nannie did not seem to care.

So we made four signs.

Then I remembered why I had gone to Nannie's room in the first place. But I decided not to talk to her about my problem. Nannie looked busy. She was tacking the signs onto the stakes so they would be easy to carry.

I sighed. Oh, well. At least I could say that I had helped someone to get ready for the parade.

I wandered downstairs. I looked out the front door. There was the Junk Bucket with its grasshopper headlights. There was Princess Emily sitting on the hood of the car.

And all over the front yard were Krushers. They had come to get their batting gloves. Kristy was handing them out proudly.

I closed the door and went upstairs to my room.

I was Karen, the jinx of the Krushers.

Bash Those Bashers!

"A cage?" Andrew was crying. "You're goint to put me in a *cage?*"

"Andrew, it is not as bad as all that," said Kristy. "You won't be locked in. You can still run out if you hit the ball."

Andrew frowned. He did not look happy. And I understood why. He was nervous.

It was the day of our practice game against the Bashers. (And it was the day of the game that would decide whether I marched with the Krushers.) The game was very important for a lot of reasons. The Krushers just *had* to do well, I thought. (That was why Andrew felt so nervous.)

Anyway, what do you think Andrew and I saw when we reached the softball field? We saw Kristy fixing something on the backstop. Bart was helping her. (Bart is the coach of the Bashers, remember?) Kristy and Bart had fastened extra pieces to each side of the backstop. The pieces were made of wood and chicken wire. They could be folded against the backstop. Or they could be swung out so the batter was standing in a sort of cage, with an opening at the front to run out of.

Right away, I knew what the cage was for: Andrew's flying bats.

"Kristy!" I complained. "Andrew will be embarrassed if he has to stand in a cage. That's not fair."

"Maybe it isn't fair," Kristy replied. "But it is safe. Andrew is still letting go of his bat. Someone might get hurt."

Andrew and I looked at each other. Andrew's eyes were full of tears.

Soon the game began.

The first time Andrew stepped into his batting cage, the Bashers laughed at him. "Baby!" they cried.

Andrew tried to ignore them. He wanted to play softball. Our cheerleaders shouted, "Bash those Bashers! Bash those Bashers!" Andrew kept his eye on the ball. He swung and missed. He also threw the bat, but at least it stayed in the cage.

However, Andrew struck out.

The Bashers did not yell at him, though. That was because Bart had yelled at the Bashers. (Andrew thanked Bart.)

It was my turn at bat. Kristy and Bart folded the extra sides away. I tried to watch the ball. But I kept thinking about Andrew and how he hated his cage. So I struck out, too.

The rest of the game did not go very well for us Krushers. But guess what? When Andrew went to bat again, he hit the ball. He threw the bat, but so what? Two players crossed home plate. Andrew had earned two runs for our team!

We still lost, though. And I struck out each time I was at bat.

When the game had ended, I marched over to Kristy. I told her about the bargain I had made with myself. "So I will not be marching with the Krushers," I said. "And I will not play in the big game. I am a jinx. I will make the Krushers lose for sure."

"Karen," said Kristy softly. "I don't care what you do about the parade. I would like you to march in it, but if you don't want to, that's okay. However, I *do* want you to play in the game. You're a part of the team. We *need* you."

"You need a jinx?"

"You are *not* a *jinx!*" exclaimed Kristy. "You're in a slump. That's all. Look. Andrew throws bats through the air. Jamie Newton ducks when the ball comes toward him. Claire Pike has tantrums. But they are all Krushers, and I want them to have the fun of playing softball. I want you to have fun, too."

"Well," I said, "maybe I will come to the big game. Maybe. And maybe I will play. *Maybe*. But I do not think I should march with the Krushers."

"Fair enough," said Kristy.

15

Dancing Nancy

*D*ing-dong!

The doorbell at the little house was ringing.

"I'll get it!" I yelled.

"Indoor voice, Karen," said Mommy from the living room.

"Sorry," I said. Then I whispered, "I'll get it."

When I reached the door, I peeked through the window. Nancy was standing on the front steps. (It is always a good idea to find out who is at your door before you open it.)

"Hi, Nancy," I said as I let her inside. I was surprised to see her. Nancy and I had not been talking to each other very much. Ever since our fight in the garage.

"Hi," replied Nancy. She smiled.

(Did that mean our fight was over?)

"What's that you're wearing?" I asked. Nancy had put on a white leotard, a gauzy white skirt with sparkles and glitter on it, white tights, and pink ballet slippers. Her hair had been combed away from her face. It was caught in a neat ponytail in back.

"What does it look like I'm wearing?" asked Nancy.

"A ballet costume."

"Right."

"How come?"

"Because this is what I've decided about the Bicycle Brigade. I am going to wear a costume. I bet most people will not think of dressing up *themselves*. They will just think of dressing up their bicycles."

"Are you going to decorate your bike, too?" I asked. "Or just yourself?"

"My bike, too. I have a really neat idea for it."

"Why are you telling me this?" I asked.

Nancy paused. She looked uncomfortable. At last she said, "I guess maybe I'm showing off. I was excited when I got this idea. I wanted to share it with you. Even if we're mad at each other, we are still best friends. . . . But you won't steal my idea, will you, Karen?"

"Of course not. I'm glad we're still friends. Anyway, you know what? I have not made up my mind about the Bicycle Brigade yet. It will depend on how well I play at our big game against the Bashers." (That was a new bargain I had made with myself.) Then I added, "Just in case I play really badly, I have been working on my bicycle some more."

"What will you buy if you win first prize?" asked Nancy.

"Silver-and-green roller blades. What will you buy?"

"I won't buy anything. Well, I won't buy anything my*self*. I will give the money to the people at Stoneybrook Manor. I will tell them that they can use it to buy some new books for their library."

"Oh," I said. Stoneybrook Manor is a very nice place. Older people move there when they can't live on their own anymore. Nancy knows a woman who stays at the Manor. She calls her Grandma B. She and Grandma B like each other very much. Grandma B is not really Nancy's grandmother. But Nancy likes to pretend she is. Nancy visits Grandma B a lot.

Buying books for the library would be gigundo nice.

Buying new roller blades when I have perfectly good roller skates would be greedy-guts. Maybe I should not be in the parade at all.

The Big Game

The next weekend was a big-house weekend. And it was a three-day weekend. So Andrew and I got to spend three days and three nights at the big house. Mommy and Seth were not even at home. They had taken a short trip to the state of Maine. (Nancy was feeding Rocky, Midgie, and my rat for them.)

On Sunday, I leaped out of bed as soon as I woke up. It was the day of the big game! I could not believe that it was already here.

I ran to Andrew's room. His bed was empty. In fact, it was made up. (I could tell that Andrew had made it himself because it was all lumpy and wrinkly.) "Andrew!" I called.

There was no answer.

I ran downstairs. Boy, was everyone excited about the game! Kristy was running all over the place. She was checking on things.

"David Michael!" she exclaimed. "How could you lose your brand-new batting glove?"

David Michael shrugged.

"Well, luckily, I have a few extras," said Kristy. "I'll give you one of those. But do *not* lose it. I don't have an endless supply."

"Okay, okay," replied David Michael. "Sheesh."

Sam was sitting at the breakfast table. Andrew was sitting across from him. "Andrew," Sam was saying, "what is a *double play*?"

"When you hit the ball and run to second base?" said my brother.

"No," said Sam patiently. "That's when you hit a double. A double *play* is when two people are put out at once. You better learn this stuff, Andrew."

Andrew squinched up his face. "I have a stomachache," he said.

Elizabeth had not been listening to the baseball discussion. But when she heard the word *stomachache*, she turned around fast.

"A tummyache?" she asked Andrew. She felt his forehead. "You don't have a fever. I think maybe you're nervous about the game today."

"Maybe," agreed Andrew.

He could not eat breakfast that morning, and neither could I — even though David Michael told us we should bulk up before the game.

An hour later, Andrew, David Michael, Kristy, and I were in our Krushers uniforms. We looked pretty good — Krushers baseball caps, T-shirts, and batting gloves, plus blue jeans and sneakers.

"Are you guys ready?" Kristy asked us.

"Yup," we replied.

"I'm glad you decided to play, Karen," she went on. "And remember, I do not expect you to hit home runs. I just want you to have fun. And to do your best. Do you understand?"

"Yes," I answered. "And I do promise to do my best." (I did not expect my best to be very good, though.)

"Okay! Everybody into the cars!" I heard Daddy call.

So all of us — my *whole* big-house family — climbed into Elizabeth's station wagon, Nannie's Pink Clinker, and Charlie's Junk Bucket. (The Junk Bucket looked halfway like a grasshopper.)

We drove to the softball field.

As soon as we got out of the cars, Andrew saw his batting cage. He began to look very determined. "Kristy," he said, "I am not going to play if you and Bart are going to cage me."

Kristy did not answer him. The Bashers had just arrived.

Winners and Losers

I always like our Krushers uniforms until I see what the Bashers are wearing. They have *real* uniforms. They have hats and gloves like ours. But instead of T-shirts and jeans, they wear the matching stripey suits like baseball players on TV. The Bashers look professional.

I am a teensy bit afraid of them.

But I could not worry about the Bashers just then. Andrew was throwing a fit. He was jumping up and down. He was shouting, "I will not go in that cage! I will not go in that cage!" He was not crying, but his face had turned dark red. It was almost purple.

"Andrew," said Kristy. "Calm down. The game is going to begin. I will have to think about the batting cage. Karen, would you and Andrew please get into batting order? We're up first."

The game began. All the Krusher fans and all the Basher fans were sitting in the bleachers. (They were mostly mommies and daddies and brothers and sisters. I wished that Mommy and Seth could watch the game, too. But they were far away in the state of Maine.)

Jackie Rodowsky was the first Krusher at bat. He swung at two pitches and missed them. ("Strike two!") Then he swung at the third pitch. He hit the ball! But it sailed out of bounds and into the bleachers.

We could hear someone yell, "Oh, gross! It smushed my hot dog!"

The Bashers laughed at Jackie. He had one more pitch left, but he missed it.

"One out!" called the umpire.

Matt Braddock was up next. He hit a double. The Krushers cheered.

David Michael hit another double. The Krushers were winning, one to nothing!

Hannie stepped up to home plate. She is not always a very good hitter. But she swung at the first pitch, whacked the ball, and started running.

"Go, Hannie, go!" yelled our cheerleaders.

The next thing we knew, Hannie had stumbled. She was sitting on the ground. She was clutching her ankle. "Ow, ow, OW!" she shrieked. Kristy, Bart, and Hannie's parents ran to her.

"It's either twisted or broken," said Mr. Papadakis grimly. He picked up Hannie and rushed her to their car. He took Hannie to the emergency room. The game had to go on without her.

"Your turn, Andrew," I said.

Andrew walked to home plate. Kristy and Bart began to swing the sides of the cage around. "No," said Andrew. "I will not play in a cage. I *promise* that I can hit without letting go of the bat."

Kristy did not know what to do. "Someone might get hurt," she said.

"No cage," repeated Andrew.

So Kristy and Bart folded back the sides. The pitcher threw the ball. Andrew swung. He missed. But the bat was still in his hands!

"Yea!" I cried.

Andrew swung two more times. He struck out. But he never let go of the bat. I was very proud of my brother.

I was also nervous. Now the Krushers had two outs, and I was up at bat. I looked at the pitcher. I looked at the ball. I watched the ball as it came toward me.

THWACK! I hit the ball and ran to first base.

Five innings later, I hit a double. I earned *two runs* for my team. In the end, the Bashers beat the Krushers, twelve to eleven. But I knew I had played well.

The next day, I would march proudly in the parade with the Krushers.

Memorial Day

I just love holidays. Like I said before, Memorial Day is not a *huge* holiday for either of my families. But when I woke up on Monday morning, I was gigundo excited.

I checked outside. The sun was shining. No clouds!

I looked at my softball uniform. I had laid it on a chair the night before.

I imagined myself marching through Stoneybrook with the Krushers.

Then I thought of the cookout. After the parade, Daddy and Elizabeth were going to have a cookout party at the big house. All of our neighbors (plus Nancy's family and Grandma B) had been invited.

I leaped out of bed and took off my nightgown. Then I put on my Krushers uniform. When I looked at myself in the mirror, I thought, Home Run Karen. I had been Home Run Karen once before. Maybe I could be her again.

How, I wondered, could I ever have thought of riding in the Bicycle Brigade? The Krushers had played very well the day before. We had *almost* beaten the Bashers. And that was gigundo hard to do.

Then I realized something. I had decorated my *little*-house bicycle for the parade. Mommy and Seth were not at home. The bicycle was locked in the garage. I could not have ridden in the Bicycle Brigade even if I had wanted to!

* * *

The parade was going to start at noon. Everyone at the big house was VERY busy in the morning. Here are some of the things that happened before my family left for the parade:

Andrew spilled orange juice down the front of his Krushers T-shirt. Nannie had to wash it and dry it *fast*. (She may have set a record.)

The grasshopper eyes fell off the front of the Junk Bucket. Charlie and Sam had to make new ones.

Kristy and Elizabeth dressed Emily to be the parade princess. At the last moment, Kristy looked at Emily and said, "Let's curl her hair."

Emily's hair is very short. But when it had been curled, and when Kristy put the crown on her head, Emily looked like . . . a real princess!

I walked her into the bathroom. I stood her in front of the mirror. "Look. There you are," I said. "You're Princess Emily."

"Tinky," said Emily Michelle. (But she was smiling.)

At eleven-thirty, Sam yelled, "Okay, everybody. We're ready to roll!"

My big-house family set off for the parade.

The Stoneybrook Parade

Downtown Stoneybrook was a mess! I had never seen so many people in one place. And most of those people were wearing costumes or uniforms.

"Where do we *go?*" I asked Daddy. I was feeling a teensy bit nervous.

"Don't worry, sweetie," said Daddy. "We'll find your places."

It took awhile, but we did. Emily stayed with Charlie in the Junk Bucket. They were waiting for the cheerleaders.

Sam saw his band and joined them.

Then Nannie spotted her bowling team. *She* joined *them*.

And then Kristy said, "Karen, Andrew, David Michael. You stay right here with me. The other Krushers will find us."

"Okay if Elizabeth and I leave now?" asked Daddy. "We want to find a good spot to watch the parade. I want perfect pictures." Daddy patted the camcorder, which was slung over his shoulder.

"It's okay," said Kristy. "I'll watch everybody."

Daddy and Elizabeth left. The Krushers began to show up. Our cheerleaders showed up, too. Guess who was almost the last Krusher to arrive. Linny Papadakis. And he was pulling Hannie in a wagon. She was wearing her uniform. Hannie had not broken her ankle. But she had twisted it — badly. Her foot was wrapped in an Ace bandage. It was so fat and puffy that she could not wear a sneaker on that foot. When she walked, she had to use crutches.

"But," Hannie said to me, "I would not

miss the parade for anything. I want every-one to know that I am a Krusher."

"Me, too," I said. I grinned at Hannie.

A few minutes later, Hannie and I heard music playing. Sam's band was leading the parade. Behind the band drove a fire truck. Behind the fire truck marched Brownies, Girl Scouts, Cub Scouts, and Boy Scouts. Then came some men in uniforms. (I am not sure who they were.)

Finally a woman walked over to Kristy. She said, "Get your team ready. You follow the Bashers."

The Bashers got to march right in front of us, all through town, carrying a sign that read: STONEYBROOK SOFTBALL CHAMPS — BART'S BASHERS.

Oh, well. I did not care too much. The people watching the parade clapped just as hard for the Krushers as they did for the Bashers.

I waved to everyone. Soon I saw Daddy and the camcorder. I waved to the cam-corder, too. I could not *wait* to see myself

on videotape that night. I could pretend that I was an actress in a TV show.

At the end of the parade route, the Krushers gathered around Kristy. We watched as the rest of the parade trickled in. There was Nannie with her bowling team. There was the Junk Bucket, carrying Charlie, Emily, and the cheerleaders. . . . And, finally, in rode the Bicycle Brigade!

I saw lots of kids I knew. And did their bicycles ever look fancy! Nancy was the only bike rider in a costume, though.

Soon after the last of the kids had ridden in, a voice blared out of a microphone. It was the judge of the Bicycle Brigade.

"I am happy to announce the winners," he began. He named the third-place winner and the second-place winner. (I did not know those kids.) And then he said, "First prize goes to Nancy Dawes."

"Yea!" I screamed. I was best friends with the contest winner! Not just anybody could say that.

Two Home Runs

Mmm. Hot dogs . . . hamburgers . . . potato salad. Good smells were everywhere. Daddy was grilling things on the barbecue. Elizabeth and Nannie carried salads out of the big house. Our neighbors came over bringing soda, juice, brownies, cookies, cakes, and ice cream.

"Hey, it's a feast!" I said to Hannie and Nancy.

"A pig-out!" added Nancy.

We giggled.

Hannie was hobbling around on her

crutches. Nancy had pinned a big blue button to her shirt. The button said: #1. Two blue ribbons hung from it. On one ribbon was written:

B
I
C
Y
C
L
E

On the other ribbon was written: BRIGADE, in the same up-and-down letters.

Grown-ups kept coming over and talking to us. To Nancy they would say, "Congratulations! It is so nice of you to give your prize to Stoneybrook Manor." To Hannie they would say, "Your poor, poor foot. I hope you will be off the crutches soon." To me they would say, "You're the baseball champ. You hit a double yesterday."

The Three Musketeers felt pretty proud.

We spent the afternoon together. First we ate lunch. We each chose two brownies, a slice of cake, a scoop of ice cream, and a soda.

"I don't think this is a balanced meal," said Hannie. But we did not care.

Later we all got in the hammock at the same time. We rocked back and forth so hard that . . . "Whoa!" cried Nancy.

The hammock tipped over and we fell out. (Nobody was hurt.)

David Michael, Linny Papadakis, Amanda and Max Delaney, Andrew, Emily, and some other kids decided to form their own Memorial Day parade. Daddy videotaped it. The Three Musketeers just watched, though. Hannie's foot was hurting, so she was sitting down. Nancy and I sat with her. The Three Musketeers belong together.

When everyone was finished eating (and digesting), Mr. Dawes called, "How about a game of softball?"

"Yes!" shouted most of the kids and some of the grown-ups.

We divided into two teams. Daddy and Mrs. Papadakis and Mr. Dawes were on my team. (I was not used to playing with grown-ups.) Mr. Dawes decided that home plate would be a tree stump, first base would be this huge oak tree, second base would be a holly bush, and third base would be an old T-shirt.

The other team was at bat first. (I was stuck in the outfield again. I tried hard to pay attention.) After two people had struck out, Andrew marched over to the tree stump.

Charlie was pitching. Sam was catching. When Sam saw Andrew with the bat, he yelled, "Everybody duck!"

A few people did.

But guess what. Andrew hit the ball with a loud *SMACK*. Then he dropped the bat gently on the ground.

He had hit a home run!

Later, when the umpire yelled, "Strike three!" the teams changed sides.

"You're up at bat first, Karen," said Daddy.

"Okay." I stood in front of the stump.

David Michael pitched to me.

I swung and . . . I hit the second home run of the game. I was Home Run Karen again.

About the Author

ANN M. MARTIN lives in New York City and loves animals. Her cat, Mouse, knows how to take the phone off the hook.

Other books by Ann M. Martin that you might enjoy are *Stage Fright*, *Me and Katie (the Pest)*, and the books in *The Baby-sitters Club* series.

Ann likes ice cream, the beach, and *I Love Lucy*. And she has her own little sister, whose name is Jane.

Little Sister

Don't miss #19

KAREN'S GOOD-BYE

"Well, I guess I better go now," said Amanda.

"I guess," I said. Amanda and I gave each other a hug. (Hannie took a few little steps back. Saying good-bye to Amanda was one thing. Hugging her was another.)

Amanda started walking backwards to the car.

"So we're really going to write, right? And will you call me sometimes, too?" said Amanda.

"Okay. And you call me," I said.

She was still walking backwards.

"Give Priscilla a pat for me," I said.

"I will," said Amanda. "Good-bye!"

"Good-bye, Amanda!" I said.

You Can Be
the Lucky BIRTHDAY KID!

Join the

BABY·SITTERS™

Little Sister

Birthday Club!

Happy Birthday to you! Join the **Baby-sitters Little Sister Birthday Club** and on your birthday, you'll receive a personalized card from Karen herself!

That's not all! Every month, a **BIRTHDAY KID OF THE MONTH** will be randomly chosen to **WIN** a complete set of *Baby-sitters Little Sister* books! The set's first book will be autographed by author Ann M. Martin!

Just fill in the coupon below. Offer expires March 31, 1992. Fill in the coupon below or write the information on a 3" x 5" piece of paper and mail to: BABY-SITTERS LITTLE SISTER BIRTHDAY CLUB, Scholastic Inc., 730 Broadway, P.O. Box 742, New York, New York 10003.

Baby-sitters Little Sister Birthday Club

❑ *YES!* I want to join the BABY-SITTERS LITTLE SISTER BIRTHDAY CLUB!

My birthday is _____

Name _____ Age _____

Street _____

City _____ State _____ Zip _____

P.S. Please put your birthday on the outside of your envelope too! Thanks!

Where did you buy this *Baby-sitters Little Sister* book?

❑ Bookstore   ❑ Drugstore   ❑ Supermarket   ❑ Library
❑ Book Club   ❑ Book Fair   ❑ Other_____(specify)
Available in U.S. and Canada only.

BLS890

The adventures continue with

THE BABY-SITTERS CLUB®

by Ann M. Martin
author of *Baby-sitters Little Sister*

If you like *Baby-sitters Little Sister*, you're going to love *The Baby-sitters Club*! Meet Karen's older stepsister Kristy and all the other club members for baby-sitting fun and excitement and adventure!

❏	NM43388-1 # 1	Kristy's Great Idea	$2.95
❏	NM43513-2 # 2	Claudia and the Phantom Phone Calls	$2.95
❏	NM43511-6 # 3	The Truth About Stacey	$2.95
❏	NM43512-4 # 4	Mary Anne Saves the Day	$2.95
❏	NM43720-8 # 5	Dawn and the Impossible Three	$2.95
❏	NM43899-9 # 6	Kristy's Big Day	$2.95
❏	NM43719-4 # 7	Claudia and Mean Janine	$2.95
❏	NM43509-4 # 8	Boy-Crazy Stacey	$2.95
❏	NM43508-6 # 9	The Ghost at Dawn's House	$2.95
❏	NM43387-3 #10	Logan Likes Mary Anne!	$2.95
❏	NM44082-9 #40	Claudia and the Middle School Mystery	$2.95
❏	NM43570-1 #41	Mary Anne vs. Logan	$2.95
❏	NM44083-7 #42	Jessi and the Dance School Phantom	$2.95
❏	NM43572-8 #43	Stacey's Emergency	$2.95
❏	NM43573-6 #44	Dawn and the Big Sleepover	$2.95
❏	NM43574-4 #45	Kristy and the Baby Parade (July)	$2.95
❏	NM43569-8 #46	Mary Anne's Revenge (August)	$2.95
❏	NM44240-6	Baby-sitters on Board! Super Special #1	$3.50
❏	NM44239-2	Baby-sitters Summer Vacation Super Special #2	$3.50
❏	NM42499-8	Baby-sitters Winter Vacation Super Special #3	$3.50
❏	NM42493-9	Baby-sitters Island Adventure Super Special #4	$3.50
❏	NM43575-2	California Girls! Super Special #5	$3.50
❏	NM43576-0	New York, New York! Super Special #6	$3.50

Available wherever you buy books, or use this order form.

Scholastic Inc., P.O. Box 7502, 2931 East McCarty Street, Jefferson City, MO 65102

Please send me the books I have checked above. I am enclosing $_____ (please add $2.00 to cover shipping and handling). Send check or money order — no cash or C.O.D.s please.

Name _____

Address _____

City _____ State/Zip _____

Please allow four to six weeks for delivery. Offer good in the U.S. only. Sorry, mail orders are not available to residents of Canada. Prices subject to change.

BSC1190